I0656335

THE
AGGRANDIZER

RAFIQ

Foreword by
Dr. Myles Bader

Printed in the United States of America

ISBN: 978-0-578-21622-5

1. Culture 2. Fiction

RAFIQ.

THE AGGRANDIZER

Disclaimer/Warning:

This book is dedicated to my ancestors for
their wisdom, strength, and endurance.

Without them, there would be no me or us.

To my children and grandchildren who
have been a great inspiration to me.

To the many people that I've met on this journey,
thank you for your positive affirmations,
which came at times when I really needed to hear a voice
from a stranger letting me know that I was on the right path.

THANK YOU!

I MUST GIVE ALL PRAISES TO THE MOST HIGH,
CREATOR OF ALL!

APDTTC.

Contents

ACT ONE   SUMMER VACATION.........................1

ACT TWO   CURIOUS TEEN........................... 9

ACT THREE   LIFE-CHANGING EXPERIENCE...............11

ACT FOUR   MEET THE WASHATON'S....................21

ACT FIVE   EACH ONE - TEACH ONE...................27

ACT SIX   THE PARTY 1........................... 39

ACT SEVEN   THE PART 11...........................47

ACT EIGHT   UTILE E'S TROUBLE.....................65

FOREWORD

This play takes place in the past and present. It is a story of a sad part of American history and the fate of many people who were deprived of living a normal life in their country of origin. It explains in very informative everyday language the plight and subsequent degradation of a race of people who were taken advantage of by a class of people that needed cheap labor to help them achieve their desired level of upper-class living.

Paying no attention to the fact that "we are all created equal," because they were "supposed to be" religious, Christian followers. They pursued monetary riches at the expense of doing extreme injustice to others.

Rafiq has done a masterful job in writing a play that I feel needs to be seen by everyone, regardless of their race or background. A play like this only comes along once in a century, written so that the meaning is easily understood and the audience will come away with a feeling for what the race has endured through the ages and their battle to gain EQUALITY!

Dr. Myles H. Bader

ACT ONE

SUMMER VACATION

SCENE ONE

EXT: FRONT PORCH - DAY

A country setting: with an old man, ERIC WASHATON, sitting in a rocking chair on his front porch enjoying the radio. A group of people approaches. They are the old man's relatives: BIG E, LITTLE E, and AQUELLAH.

ERIC

Watch out now! Who's that? Do I know y'all? Hey there! Yep, yep, yep, ye...

BIG E, interrupts the old man in the middle of his "yep fest."

BIG E

Daddy, daddy! That's enough yeps man, ooo wee!

BIG E looks at LITTLE E shaking his head and laughing.

BIG E

You are going to have an interesting summer!

BIG E hugs the old man and inhales a big chest-full of air.

BIG E

Man, there's nothing like this fresh country air.

ERIC
(Snickering)

You can't run for the country mayor!

BIG E
(Low voice)

I didn't say I was running for mayor! I said I like this fresh country air!

ERIC

Yep, yep, yep, yep, I remember...did I tell y'all about the time my best friend James sneaks his way into Benedict Arnold's camp a...

BIG E
(Interrupting)

Yes, yes, you've told me that story at least a million times.

AQUELLAH

Benedict Arnold? How old are you daddy?

ERIC

Weelll, let's see here. I was born November 14 in the 1880s at sunrise, 5:30 in the A.M. In thu 1880s I ain't gone tell ya when.

AQUELLAH

The 1880s, good Lord! I bet there's a lot of history in your head.

BIG E

Don't get him started. We don't have time to hear it all (again) *anyway.*

ERIC Note: Since the old man was hard of hearing, he proceeded to tell the story.

ERIC

Yep, I remember back in 1895 when James served under General George Washington himself. He...

BIG E interrupts.

BIG E

(Kissing the old man on his forehead)

Daddy, daddy, we're leaving now. We'll see you in a few weeks when we come back to pick up LITTLE E. We love you!

AQUELLAH

(She kisses him on the cheek)

I'll listen to one of your stories the next time we come down.

AQUELLAH AND BIG E exit the stage waving to LITTLE E and the old man.

LITTLE E

Well, it's just you and me granddaddy. I'll be more than happy to listen to your stories. It seems as though father is always so busy these days working in his "secret laboratory" in his basement.

LITTLE E starts walking downstage.

LITTLE E

I don't understand father sometimes granddaddy. He's so brilliant! He's always inventing things and using his mind to try and help better our lives. But he still won't let me be a part of that side of his life.

LITTLE E

(Holds his head low then looks up toward the sky)

I wish he would share his dreams with me.

He turns to his granddaddy who has not heard a word he has said. He kneels down in front of the rocking chair like a child and waits for another history lesson from the old man.

LITTLE E

O.K. Granddaddy, tell me all about your friend, James and General Washington.

The old man proceeds to tell the story as the curtain closes.

CURTAIN

SCENE TWO

INT: FATHER'S (BIG E) HOME, LIVING ROOM

LITTLE E returns home to his father's house. They are in the living room. Music is playing. BIG E and his son are having a tepid conversation.

BIG E

Son, don't press me on this. You know why you are not allowed in the basement.

LITTLE E

(Using his hands to emphasize his feelings)

But father that accident I had in your lab was eleven years ago. I was a child then! I'm a grown man now! I want to be part of your life and help in any way I can. Why are you being so difficult about this?

BIG E

(Pacing back and forth, hands on his hips)

I don't mean to shut you out, son. It's just that this invention will be the greatest achievement in the history of the world. (Excitedly) *Nothing! Absolutely nothing has come close to this, and I don't want to talk about it to anyone! Not even your mother knows about it.*

He walks to his son and puts his hands on his son's shoulder, and in a calmed-down voice explains.

BIG E (CONT'D)

You and your mother are the most important things in my life. You may not think so right now, but you must believe that what I am doing is for you and her. I'm on the threshold of something so fantastic that I have trouble believing myself the possibilities of it all.

(He looks off with a wandering mind....the possibilities of it all.)

LITTLE E
(Acts frustrated)

I do understand why you feel you have to protect this project, but why can't I help? I can take notes or just be a gopher or something! Anything father!

BIG E

Let me think about it for a while son and I'll let you know.

LITTLE E
(Excitedly)

O.K. O.K. That's better than no!

BIG E

I SAID THAT I WOULD THINK ABOUT IT! But in the meantime, stay away from my lab (he points his finger at LITTLE E and shakes it)...*STAY OUT OF THE BASEMENT, SON!*

LITTLE E

I hear ya, Dad!

BIG E

I have to go into town for some supplies. Tell your mother for me.

LITTLE E nods his head and watches his father leave the room.

BIG E
(Offstage)

Remember what I said, son!

LITTLE E puts his hands in his pockets and holds his head down, acting like a child that has just been caught with his hand in the cookie jar.

CURTAIN

ACT TWO

CURIOUS TEEN

SCENE ONE

INT: BASEMENT - BIG E HOME

LITTLE E enters the lab. He is amazed by all that he sees. There are papers scattered everywhere, electronic equipment and a large canister-shaped device that has an open door and a lighted display that reads "1800." (Talking to himself) What in the world is this? What is dad working on?

LITTLE E walks around the machine with his mouth hanging open. He spots some papers with some diagrams drawn on them. He sorts through them in order to find some clue as to what his father is up to and why all the secrecy.

LITTLE E
(Talking low and out loud)

What is this (sorting through the papers)? *I can't make heads nor tails of this...but...wait...*(his eyes get big). *No, it can't be...can it? Is this what Dad is working on? A time machine! No ...nooo, that's impossible!*

Is Dad just crazy? Has he lost his mind? Oooo, the man needs some mental counseling if he really believes that he can invent something as revolutionary .....no, something as inconceivable as a time machine. DAMN! My father is a "MADMAN!"

LITTLE E has the papers in his hands as he walks to the "Aggrandizer." He looks at the papers and laughs.

LITTLE E
(Still talking out loud)

He even has a name for this contraption. (He lowers his voice and says sarcastically) *"THEEE AG-GRAND-IZER!"* (He becomes comical with his body movements)," *Yess, ladies and gentlemen, I give you the "The Aggrandizer," a time machine!*

There will be one in every home in the next ten years. Go to your local Kmart and pick one up! One for you and one for your kids! (He becomes serious) *Dad, what are you doing?* (He goes inside the Aggrandizer).

LITTLE E
(Coming out of Aggrandizer, talking)

This looks impressive I must say!

He goes back in and shuts the door. There is smoke (fog) in the machine. LITTLE E tries to open the door...but can't. All of a sudden he is gone.

CURTAIN - BLACKOUT

ACT THREE

LIFE-CHANGING EXPERIENCE

SCENE ONE

EXT; COTTON FIELD - 1800's

LITTLE E is in a field with cotton, hay, a barn in the distance, and people in the field. They are dressed poorly. The men are tattered and torn, the women have rags tied around their heads, and some are carrying baskets. There is a white man with a whip, and he is yelling at the people.

LITTLE E is mesmerized. He is behind a stack of hay.

He stays there out of sight until he gets his thoughts together. He only knows that a few seconds ago he was in his father's lab...now he is in an open field with some strangely-dressed people and a white man with a whip.

LITTLE E
(Talking out loud in a low voice)

Where the fuck am I? Who are those people? (He stays low) *They almost look like...SLAAAVES!! This is not happening! This... cannot... be... real! I must be asleep or something!*

Something catches his attention. The people in the field are coming closer. The white man with the whip starts beating one of the slaves mercilessly. He is screaming all kinds of obscenities to the slave. His name is PERCY, the overseer to the slaves. He comes around to the other side of the group of slaves and commences to whip one of the slave women. His back is too LITTLE E at this point.

PERCY

You lazy black bastards!! Work FASTER!! Y'alls been in dis field all fuckin' day! Git a move on!! I hate all y'all and I's is go she' y'all how much I hate ya!! He draws his whip back striking a female slave.

LITTLE E can't stand it anymore.

LITTLE E

OH, HEELLL NO!!

(Leaping from behind the hay, he attacks PERCY, knocking him to the ground. PERCY is out cold.) The slaves could not believe their eyes! A black man that dared to strike a white man! They are all quiet and look at LITTLE E as though he was from another planet. One slave named NOBIE grabs LITTLE E by the arm.

NOBIE

I's go hide ya now, boy. He go kill ya when he wake up. I's hide ya in da barn.

CURTAIN

SCENE TWO

INT: BARN - 1800's

They are all in the barn now. PERCY never saw who hit him. He came to the barn with a warning to the slaves.

PERCY

I's don't know which one of you niggras hit me, but I's find out and when I does, all y'all asses is gonna pay!

PERCY exits the barn.

NOBIE then signals for LITTLE E to come out. The slaves are all mesmerized by LITTLE E.

NOBIE

You's a different kind lookin' nigga, but we's glad to see ya.

The other slaves are TEVIN, NIC, and the "SINGING SLAVE."

NOBIE
(Talking to the other slaves)

NIC, TEVIN, SINGIN', look at them duds, dis nigga be wearrin'!

NIC

Look at da fancy gold fixin's!

TEVIN
(Pointing to LITTLE E's watch)

What dat be on ya arm?

LITTLE E

It's a watch. Haven't you ever seen a watch before?

NIC

He don't sound like no black boy I's ever heard talk.

13

NOBIE

Who's nigga ya be? Fancy duds, gold wit perty glass in it, mus' be from some fancy plantation, up norf maybe.

LITTLE E

Number one, I'm nobody's "niggra." I'm not a slave... at least not as you know slavery...

They all have a puzzled look on their faces.

LITTLE E

Where in the hell am I?

NOBIE

You's be in Jackson, Mississipp, on MASSA WASHATON's plantation. What plantation you's come from?

LITTLE E

I told you that I am not a slave, nor do I come from any plantation. I was born in Kansas City, Missouri, November 14, 1996. Where I come from, there is no more slavery. All black men are free! But my father's name is Washaton and so was my grandfather and my great-grandfather's.

They were born in Jackson, Mississippi. They both used to tell me stories about being involved with slavery. I wonder... (LITTLE E starts to realize that his father's invention works), *could this be my father's plantation? Are there any other Washaton's plantations around here?*

NOBIE

Not dat I's knows of.

LITTLE E
(Excited)

Dad, oh Dad!! It works! My soul, it works! The Aggrandizer works, Dad! You're a genius!!

The slaves look at him as though he were a crazy man.

TEVIN

How we sho'ou ain't stealin''round here? dat nigga who be

NIC

Hush up dat! Tain't no white man 'round here got no thangs like he be havin'. Ain't never seen no britches like dem or no shoes like dat. I's think he's ain't from no where 'round here! I's think he's some kinda spirit dat comes to set us's free!

LITTLE E

No, I am not some kind of Messiah or deliverer sent from heaven. I'm a man, just like all of you (raises leg and hand, and he paces back and forth). *What year is this?*

NOBIE

I'm not know the year. But I's done know we's in da 1800s.

LITTLE E

DAMN! The 1800s! How am I going to get back to my own time? (He turns to NOBIE.) *I have to find my grandfather. He must be here on the plantation. His name is ERICSTON WASHATON. Do you know where he is?*

NOBIE

I's not know.

LITTLE E

Who lives in the big house?

NOBIE

Da Massa, he wife, da house niggas, and da slave dat stay in da top of da house.

LITTLE E

Top of the house, what do you mean?

NOBIE

(He points to the house and shows LITTLE E
the light coming from the attic)

Yeah, come see. See dat light up yonder?

LITTLE E

*Oh, you mean the attic. There's someone living
up there?*

NOBIE

*Yeah, a field nigga, but he never in da field. Tain't
never seen him in da field. Tain't never seen him
outside in da day. I's seen him when it be dark. I's
sneaked back from da utha barn where da women's be and
I's sees Massa and da field nigga comes outta da house
one night.*

*Dey sits on da porch and da nigga boy, he sit in da
Massa's wife porch swing. Dat swing fo' white folk
only! Dis nigga even dressed like Massa; even smokin'
a pipe like Massa. I's saw Massa gives him da fire.*

LITTLE E

Are you sure this is what you saw?

NOBIE

I's sho' !

LITTLE E

*You know what! I will bet my life that is my great-
grandfather in that attic. White people don't treat
black people that way or any other people of color
unless there is something in it for them.*

NOBIE

*If dat be yo great-granpappy, why is he in da
Massa's roof?*

LITTLE E

*How can I make you understand without confusing the
fuck out of you? Listen...my great grandfather was an
inventor. Do you know what an inventor is?*

They all shake their heads NO!

LITTLE E (CONT'D)

*O.K. An inventor is someone who makes things or builds
something to make our lives easier.*

LITTLE E (CONT'D)

(LITTLE E proceeds to show the slaves an example of a
20th- century invention, the dustpan)

*Let's say.... you want to sweep up this pile of dirt
and throw it away. Now, the only way to get it up is
with your hands, right! So, I invent something to help
you put the pile of trash into the trashcan faster.
Follow me?*

NOBIE

Where ya be goin'?

LITTLE E

(Shaking his head in disbelief)

*Aaa...never mind. Just pay attention and watch. O.K. I
have the trash all in a pile. Now,* (he grabs an empty
basket for the trashcan) *I am going to throw the trash
away. This basket will be the trashcan.*

In order to clean up this pile of trash (LITTLE E uses
exaggerated movements to show the slaves what he means)
*we have to pick it up with our hands after we sweep
it all up. But, if we had something to sweep the trash*

onto and pick it up that way, it would be much easier
for you to throw it away and it would cut your work
time in half.

LITTLE E looks around for something to serve as a dustpan.
He finds a flat piece of torn basket.

LITTLE E (CONT'D)

Now! Let's sweep the trash up this flat piece of basket.
See how much easier and faster it is to do it this way
instead of picking it up with just your hands?

The slaves just stare at LITTLE E for a second and NOBIE
smiles.

NOBIE

Dat do be faster.

LITTLE E

My great-grandfather must have invented something, and
that's why he is kept away from the other slaves. I
have got to find out why he's being kept in the attic.
I have to get into the house without being seen.

NIC

Da Massa leave at da end of da day, and he be gone
long spell.

LITTLE E

How long is a long spell?

NIC

He be gone one sundown to's da next'in.

LITTLE E

Perfect! I'll try and sneak in tonight.

NOBIE

'Members, da Massa's wife be home, and maybe da chillin's be home.

LITTLE E

Don't worry; I'll be careful.

CURTAIN

ACT FOUR

Meet The Washaton's

SCENE ONE

INT: DINING ROOM - MASTER WASHATON'S HOME - EVENING

MASTER WASHATON'S dining room. They, MASTER WASHATON and his wife, MRS. WASHATON, are having dinner. It is the evening time.

MASTER WASHATON

How's things been goin' 'round here lately? Where the chil'res?

MRS. WASHATON

Around somewheres.

MASTER WASHATON

I'm gonna go and round up some horses tonight, so don't wait up for me.

MRS. WASHATON

(Agitated)

Don't you mean round up some niggra bitches?

MASTER WASHATON

There will be none of that kind of talk at MY dinner table!!

MRS. WASHATON

It's MY table too! And I'll say what I damn well please to you!

MASTER WASHATON gets up from his chair, walks to MRS. WASHATON (she cowers a little) and backhand slaps her from her chair.

MASTER WASHATON

Now, go to yo' room bitch, until ya learns to respect me in MY house!

MRS. WASHATON grabs her face and runs from the room crying like a little girl. MASTER WASHATON exits the room in a huff.

CURTAIN

SCENE TWO

INT: MRS. WASHATON'S BEDROOM - EVENING

She is changed for bed. MASTER WASHATON is gone for the evening. LITTLE E has gotten into the house and is trying to get to the attic. He has to pass by MRS. WASHATON'S room. He tries to sneak past the bedroom door but is seen by the love-starved MRS. WASHATON.

MRS. WASHATON

Hey boy!! What you doin' in here? I ain't seen you befo'e. You that new slave just been bought?

LITTLE E

(Thinking fast)

Yes, ma'am.

MRS. WASHATON

What cha say? You don't talk like no slave boy. Where you from?

LITTLE E

Aa...I's ain't no different from the utha nigga's ma'am.

MRS. WASHATON

I could have sworn you almost sound like a white man. But, what cha doin' in the house?

LITTLE E

I's jest lost ma'am. I's lookin' fo' MASSA WASHATON.

MRS. WASHATON

Well, he ain't here.

(She becomes seductive. She doesn't really care
why LITTLE E is in the house. All she wants is
to make love with this fine slave)

Were you watching me boy?

LITTLE E knows what is up with MRS. WASHATON and plays along.

LITTLE E

Oh! No, ma'am! I's not watchin' ya, ma'am!

MRS. WASHATON

Don't lie boy! You knows you want me! Come here! (She beckons him to her bed and at the same time rubbing herself all over). *You ever been wit a white woman befo'e boy?*

LITTLE E

(Acting to the hilt)

I's ain't never seent no white woman in da flesh befo'e, ma'am.

MRS. WASHATON

(Grabbing LITTLE E's private parts)

Well, it's about time ya did.

She proceeds to kiss LITTLE E and takes off his shirt. She removes her clothes.

MRS. WASHATON

What's that in yo' britches? You done stole somethin' boy?

LITTLE E

No, ma'am. I's ain't stole nuttin'. Dat's me in da britches!

MRS. WASHATON

DAMNATION!!

LITTLE E and MRS. WASHATON engage in sex. Everything goes black to show that some time has elapsed. After they finish, MRS. WASHATON has the biggest smile on her face.

MRS. WASHATON

You bet not let my husband find out you was in this house, boy. He'll whip the shit outta ya or might even hang ya. So, nigga boy, you come back here tomorrow night 'bout this same time. You the best nigga I done had yet! Be here boy, ya hear me?

LITTLE E

Yes'em, Massa's wife!!

CURTAIN

ACT FIVE

Each One - Teach One

SCENE ONE

INT: BARN - NIGHTTIME

Back in the barn; the same night. LITTLE E comes back into the barn.

NOBIE
Did'ja see yo great-granpappy? What'cha find out?

LITTLE E
I found out that the master's wife is a love starved freak!

NOBIE
(Looking puzzled)

Huh?

LITTLE E
I mean she likes to have sex with black men!

NOBIE
You didn't fool wit da Massa's wife, did'ja?

LITTLE E
(Mimicking NOBIE)

Damn right I did fool wit the Massa's wife!

TEVIN

What it be like? A white woman different from a nigga woman?

LITTLE E

Hey! I want you all to stop calling each other "nigga!" That's a terrible name that white people call us because they believe that we are no more than animals! It's an ugly word that puts you down as men! YOU... ARE...MEN! NOT NIGGERS!!

>   With rage in his voice, he begins to
>   preach and frighten the slaves.

YES!! I FUCKED THE MASSA'S WIFE!! JUST LIKE THE WHITE MAN HAS FUCKED OUR WOMEN AND FUCKED OVER THE BLACK MAN! MAKING HIM BELIEVE THAT WE ARE NOT AS GOOD AS THEY ARE AND THAT WE HAVE NO MIND THAT IS CAPABLE OF CREATING OR THINKING; THAT WE ARE NOT INTELLIGENT OR DESERVING OF THE FINER THINGS IN LIFE!

(He calms down) *I am going to teach all of you to read, write, count, and to think for yourselves. I will teach you as much as possible. Do you want to learn?*

They all nod YES!

LITLE E

Good! What happens here hopefully will change the outcome for the black man in this world.

LITTLE E (CONT'D)

The abominate superintends have had their way long enough. We must unite and take back what is rightfully ours. We have been stripped of our dignity, our inventions, our culture, we have been pitted against each other, and the only gains that we have made in this universe are the ones that "they" gave to us. We have no power; no real say-so on how things are ran in our government, we are a divided race that is headed toward systematic elimination... (he pauses and looks into the eyes of the slaves...)

I'll talk to all of you some more later, but for now, I need to get back into the house. I just hope...that I can get past the master's horneyass wife.

NOBIE

You's best ta wait till da 'morrow, when it be dark ag'in. Da Massa go' haves a buncha udda white folks ta visit he and he wife den. Dey go' be sangin,' dancin', and pickin' da fiddle. You's go in da house den.

LITTLE E

(Jokingly, but yet frustrated.)

Man, your vocabulary is so wack! But, you're right. I'll wait until tomorrow. We need to get some sleep.

They all get ready to bed down for the night.

CURTAIN - BLACKOUT

SCENE TWO

INT: BARN - MORNING

In the barn the next morning, NOBIE tells LITTLE E about what to expect on a typical workday in the fields. He also tells LITTLE E about the snitch named SKULLY.

NOBIE

Tis go be a ruffin' dis day. PERCY go beat we's real hard. He go try'n make we's tell who hit him yesterday.

NIC

Yeah, he go be real hot t'day. I's hope we's git some new girl slaves, so PERCY have somethin' ta do and won't beats we's all da day.

LITTLE E

What do you mean; some new girl slaves? What does that have to do with PERCY beating any of you?

NOBIE

He mean dat if'n PERCY got somethin' else ta thanks 'bout, he don't be beatin' on we's so much. He likes the new slave women dat come. He always gits some fo'he self.

LITTLE E
(Disgusted)

That's bullshit! PERCY will get his white ass kicked from here to kingdom come if I have anything to say about it! I'll teach that pot bellied, Skoal-dippin', goat-smelling, hillbilly vittle-cookin', black woman rapin', redneck peckerwood, not to disrespect our black queens!!

NIC

*Ya knows dat da Massa's wife be huntin' fo' ya tanite.
You's done made her happy!*

LITTLE E

How do you know that I made her happy last night?

NOBIE

*Coz, if'n you did'nt, she tells Massa you's teched
her and the Massa have you's hung. (NOBIE smiles)
Her was happy!*

LITTLE E

*Oh well! I'll worry about that later. I just want to
get through this day and get back into that house.*

NOBIE

*I's got's ta tells ya 'bout dat nigga, SKULLY. He be
Massa's bestest nigga. He sees all and he tell all ta
Massa. We's never sees SKULLY, but he's 'round to tell
ever'time somethin' happen. SKULLY know.*

LITTLE E

*Thanks, NOBI. Don't worry. I won't let an "Uncle Tom"
like SKULLY stop me from doing what I have to do.*

NOBIE

*Who be "Uncle Tom?" He be in da Massa's roof wit yo'
great-grandpappy.*

LITTLE E just has this perplexed look on his face. He shakes
his head and smiles.

LITTLE E

*Aaa...yeah...I'll tell you all about "Uncle Tom"
NOBIE. For now, I guess we better get into the field.
(He remembers something.) Oh, tell me more about this
party that the master is having tonight. Will there be
a lot of people?*

NOBIE

OOOO WEEEEE! Yessah! They's comes from all plantations. TEVIN he be turnin' flips 'n' dancin' 'n' SINGIN be sangin...

LITTLE E interrupts sarcastically.

LITTLE E

SINGIN be sangin'?

NOBIE

(Laughing)

Sho' nuff! Mos' everybody go be outside 'n' da yard. Ain't too many folks, 'n' da house. Dat be jest good fo' ya ta sneaks in da house whilst all dem white folks laughin' wit TEVIN.

LITTLE E

(Angrily)

You mean laughing?!! TEVIN? Oh, my brothers, I can't wait to wake you all up!

LITTLE E and the rest of the slaves prepare to go into the field. SKULLY enters the barn. SKULLY, looking around and fixing his eyes on LITTLE E.

SKULLY

Where dis nigga come from? I's ain't seen him 'round here befo'e. I's could be's wrong. I's thank I's seent you's jest yistaday.

LITTLE E

(His eyes following SKULLY's every move.)

What do you want?

SKULLY

(Surprised at LITTLE E's diction)

You's ain't no nigga from 'round here! Massa will like to talk ta a nigga likes you. PERCY might wants a word or two wit y'all, too...

LITTLE E grabs SKULLY around his neck and throws him to the ground. SKULLY can't get loose. LITTLE E has him in a wrestling hold.

LITTLE E

(Scuffling with SKULLY)

Let me tell your Uncle-Tom-ass something! You breathe a word to MASTER WASHATON about me and I'll break every bone in your neck; I'll crack your back in 18 different places; I'll tear your arm off at the roots and shove it up your stupid black ass!!

DO...YOU...FUCKING...UNDERSTAND...ME?

SKULLY

(Amazed and dazed)

YESSAH!! YESSAH!!

SKULLY jumps up and runs out of the barn. The others laugh and cheer as SKULLY runs away.

TEVIN

OOO WEEE!! Dat nigga sho' kin run!!

CURTAIN

SCENE THREE

INT: BARN AFTER DAYS WORK - NEAR SUNDOWN

The slaves are tired and so is LITTLE E.

LITTLE E

Man! I'm tired as hell! Our people have been doing this shit for hundreds of years for free.

(He falls down on the nearest soft surface)

This is straight out BULLSHIT and before I leave here, if I get to leave here, they will have to kill me because I am not with this program and all those that listen to me and learn to use their own minds to think for themselves will realize that this is so wrong. No man deserves to be treated this way.

NOBIE

Ys say "free labor," what dat mean?

LITTLE E

It means not getting paid any money or some other form of compensation for your work. That's not right! When we work for no wages or the promise of land, we only the white man to prosper on our backs. He reaps all the money and the land for himself and give you nothing but a tongue-lashing and the whip.

In the worst of cases, all you end up with is a rope around your neck, a bullet in your head or back, or death by burning. The white man has always treated people of color with no dignity or respect. They feel that we are less than animals. They treat their dogs a hell-a-va lot better than they will ever treat you.

NIC

Udda colors of people? Whatcha mean? Taint no udda colors of peoples, jest we's 'n' white folks. I's thank ya been out 'n' da sun too long. Heats gone to ya head I's reckon.

LITTLE E

(Mocking NIC)

Heat's done gone to ya head I's reckon! There are at least three families of color on this earth, my man!

LITTLE E (CONT'D)

There is the red man, also known as the Indian, who was on this land before the white man took it all from him. There is the black man, who came from Africa, through no choice of his own, and the yellow man that came from Asia.

The white man came from Europe eventually, but not originally. I say that because of the scientist, Yakub's experiment. I don't have time to teach you about that right now, but I will teach you so much before I leave.

NIC

(Loud and eyes bucked)

I's thank you's done gone 'n' lose ya mind!! Taint no sucha thang, a man wit red skin on he body 'n' a yella man! Taint nevva seent nunna dem colors you's talkin' 'bout. Jest black'ns 'n' white'ns!

LITTLE E

(Louder and frustrated)

And do you know why you've never seen another man of color besides the black man and the white man? Because your country-ass has never been anywhere except on this God-forsaken plantation.

The white man's government hasn't begun to let these other people of color into this country in large quantities yet. There are so many nationalities of people in this world NIC that you haven't a clue as to how many.

One day your children and grandchildren will meet other people of color and different cultures, and it can happen sooner than you think, if only I could help to wake all of you up out of this hellish nightmare... (realizing that he is not going to change anyone's mind right now)*... but enough of this. I need to get back into that house. Where does SKULLY sleep?*

NIC

He stay 'n' da chicken coop right next ta Massa's house. He peep all da time at da Massa's chillins 'n' he do dad a Massa's woman. Massa don't kno' dat doe.

LITTLE E

Where is WASHATON when his wife is fooling around with the slaves?

NOBIE

Him gone ta catch dem runnin' slaves 'n' brang'em back here.

LITTLE E

Oh yeah! That punk-ass bitch! I'm going my size 11's in that motherfucker's ass before I leave here!

NIC

Whatcha call Massa?

LITTLE E

(Hands on his hips)

He's a punk-ass, motherfukin', redneck, goat smellin,' funny-walkin', slave-ownin,' BASTARD!! Anyway! I need to know what time that country fuck is leaving. Do you know what time that may be, NOBIE? Oh damn! I forgot that you guys can't tell time; probably can't count either.

NOBIE

Count! What dat?

LITTLE E

I'll teach all of you how to count. I'll start you with the basic one plus one equals two.

ACT SIX

The Party 1

SCENE ONE

INT: 2018 MASTER WASHATON'S HOME - SPLIT STAGE 2018 &
BARN 1800s

BIG E is celebrating his birthday and wondering where his
son may be. While back in the 1800s, LITTLE E is ~~teaching~~
the slaves all that he possibly can. They are surprisingly
quick learners. BIG E is entertaining his guests.

There is 70s music playing with a variety of other types of
music. There is a live D.J., JOE LAROCCA, who is mixing and
laughing at the way everyone is dancing.

BIG E

Where is LITTLE E?

AQUELLAH

*I don't know sweetheart. I haven't seen him since
yesterday. That's strange...I know he wouldn't miss
your birthday like this unless...*

BIG E

Unless what?

AQUELLAH

(Not wanting to seem worried)

Oh, I just mean that he must be busy doing something else that would cause him to miss your birthday.

BIG E

What could be more important than my birthday?

AQUELLAH

Nothing dear!

BIG E

Nothing is right!

AQUELLAH just smiles and shakes her head. BIG E goes to his other guests and mingles with them. When a James Brown song starts playing, BIG E grabs his wife and starts doing some unidentifiable dance. He is feeling pretty good and is embarrassing AQUELLAH with his dancing.

BIG E

Come on AQUELLAH!! Shake it up, shake it up! You know that I was the best dancer around in the day!

BIG E does the James Brown shuffle.

AQUELLAH

Now, you know you need to quit! You look like your having a seizure!

BIG E

AAAH! Come on girl! You know that you can't hang with the master!!

AQUELLAH

Master! Yeah, of disaster!

BIG E

Well, show us what you got then!

AQUELLAH

What our nutty professor!

AQUELLAH starts to dance around BIG E. She is shimmering and shaking while everyone is laughing. BIG E joins her.

BIG E

That' it, that's it! Watch out for the original Soul Train dancers...comin' through!!

Everyone forms a line, and each of them dance down to downstage, doing some kind of hilarious dance steps. They are all whooping and hollering and egging each other on.

PARTY GUEST

Man! You guys look like drunken penguins!

BIG E

The Penguin! Yeah! I remember that one!

BIG E breaks out doing the Penguin. Everybody is laughing and naming off different dances.

PARTY GUEST II

Cold Duck! Remember that one?

AQUELLAH

Hell yes! That was one of my favorites!

AQUELLAH breaks out doing the Cold Duck.

PARTY GUEST III

Aaahhh! Sookie, Sookie now!

The PARTY GUESTS, BIG E and AQUELLAH ham it up with their dancing prowess. (The lights dim on the party).

INT: BARN - LIGHTS GETTING BRIGHTER - DIM ON THE PARTY.

While the party is going on in 2018, back in the 1800s, LITTLE E is in the barn teaching the slaves to count and to read.

LITTLE E

... and watch my motions NOBIE. This is the letter "N."

NOBIE

"N."

LITTLE E

That's a good man! The second letter is called an "Q."

NOBIE

"Q."

LITTLE E

Good, good! The next letter is "B."

NOBIE

"B's."

LITTLE E

No, no. Not "B's," just say "B."

LITTLE E

Excellent! You men are fast learners! This is going to be great!

The lights dim in the barn scene and come back up in the party scene. BIG E and AQUELLAH have danced and laughed themselves into exhaustion.

CURTAIN

SCENE TWO

INT: PARTY - BIG E HOUSE

As the curtain reopens, everyone at the party is just lying around, and some of the guests are leaving. BIG E and AQUELLAH are escorting some people to the door.

BIG E

Good night folks and thanks for coming.

AQUELLAH

I hope that BIG E'S dancing didn't scare you!

BIG E

Aahh, wait a minute now! Your dancing wasn't exactly the most gracefully executed movements I've ever seen either!

AQUELLAH

(She starts to walk away)

Shut up, mere mortal!

BIG E runs up behind her and gooses her in the side. She falls over laughing. He hugs her and kisses her and then has a worried look on his face.

AQUELLAH

What's wrong sweetie? LITTLE E?

BIG E

Yes, LITTLE E, where is he?

The lights dim on the party and the lights in the barn come on.

INT: BARN - LIGHTS COME ON

LITTLE E

O.K.! TEVIN, what's one plus one?

TEVIN
(Excited)

TWOOO!!

LITTLE E

All right!!! Great! I'M SO PROUD OF YOU MAN! Way to go! Well, fellows, it's getting late. We better call it a night and get some sleep.

They all moan in disappointment.

NOBIE

I's...I mean...I ain't sleepy. Want ta learn some mo'.

LITTLE E

All in due time my man. Right now we all really need to hit the hay. It's going to be a long day tomorrow. Even though there are so many things that I want to tell you all about ... cars, trains, computers, television, radio, CD's, records, video games and garbage disposals.

Starter jackets, Michael Jordon, Michael Jackson, Jesse Jackson, Air Jordon tennis shoes...aaa...aaa... uh, Nintendo, and SEGAi!

Ford, General Motors...man, my mind is just buzzin' with all these things!! Oh yeah!!

Bubbalicious!! Tacos!! MICKEY D's...Damn! I got to go to sleep! Tomorrow...tomorrow you'll learn some more.

The slaves are all happy and giggling like school children. They all are sitting and staring at LITTLE E.

LITTLE E
(Noticing how they are staring)

WHAT! Why are you all looking at me like that? Do I have shit on my shoes or something?

NOBIE

We jest taint nevva heard no black man talks da way you does….

LITTLE E

Hey! What did I tell you about that "we's" stuff?

NIC

Don't say we's, say we.

LITTLE E

RIGHT! RIGHT! You catch on real fast, NIC! Now, let's get some sleep.

They all move to their respective sleeping areas and bed down. TEVIN talks as the lights dim.

TEVIN

ONE PLUS ONE...IS...TWOOO!!

LITTLE E

You are just too cool, TEVIN. Good night everybody.

Everyone says "good night."

INT: BIG E HOUSE - LIGHTS COME ON

The lights come up in 2018. BIG E and AQUELLAH are bidding their last guest goodnight.

PARTY GUEST

(Slightly plastered, stumbling out the door)

'Nite all. Great time, greeeaaat time! Leva ya!

BIG E

Thanks for coming.

BIG E shuts the door and he and AQUELLAH sit on the couch.

AQUELLAH

Well, who is going to clean up this mess?

BIG E

It's my birthday, remember? I'm on vacation.

They both laugh.

AQUELLAH
(She rubs BIG E on his back)

I'm going to turn in now because I am a little intoxicated. Don't worry about LITTLE E. I'm sure he had a good reason for not being here.

BIG E

I know baby. It's not as though he were still a little child. He's a grown man, and I have to respect that.

They kiss each other, and AQUELLAH bids BIG E goodnight.

AQUELLAH

How long are you going to stay up?

BIG E

Oh, I think that I will do a little work in the lab before I turn in.

AQUELLAH
(Turning to leave)

I should have known. You won't even take your birthday off when it comes to that lab! I love you anyway. Don't be too long.

BIG E

All right!!

ACT SEVEN

The Part 11

SCENE ONE

INT: LAB - BASEMENT

BIG E is in the lab. Upon entering he notices that someone has been in the lab going through his papers. He walks quickly around checking everything.

BIG E
(Out loud)

Someone has been in here!

He sprints over to the Aggrandizer. The door is shut. He immediately knows that someone has been tampering with the machine. He knows that it could have only been his son.

BIG E
(He scoops up some papers from the floor)

NO!! NO!! LITTLE E!! WHAT HAVE YOU DONE? SON! WHAT HAVE YOU DONE?

BIG E falls to the floor in a heap. He is shaking his head in disbelief. He finally composes himself and rises.

BIG E
(Holding the papers tightly to his chest)

I have to get you back son...wherever you are?

The lights dim in the lab while BIG E is sorting through his papers.

INT: BARN - LIGHTS COME UP

It is the next day for the slaves, another day in the field. They all worked to nightfall. When they enter the barn, they are exhausted. LITTLE E sees another opportunity to sneak into the house. MASTER WASHATON's party is going full force. Almost all of his guests are drunk or passed out.

NIC

Now dat Massa's white folk dancin' 'n' sangin,' you can get to ya grandpappy.

LITTLE E

Yeah, I've got to get into that attic this time.

LITTLE E looks outside the barn door to see if it is clear.

LITTLE E

O.K., everybody. I'm going to need your help. I just need you all to watch out for PERCY or any other white people that might come this way.

NOBIE

We...got...yo...back, homey!

LITTLE E bursts out laughing.

LITTLE E

YO! DOG!! You got my back! ALRIIIGHT!!

LITTLE E laughs all the way out the door.

CURTAIN

SCENE TWO

INT: ATTIC

A young black man is sitting at a desk. There arebundles of papers everywhere. He is LITTLE E's grandfather, ERICSTON WASHATON.

INT: OFFSTAGE - LITTLE E KNOCKS ON THE DOOR INT: ATTIC

ERICSTON opens the door. There stands LITTLE E, speechless. LITTLE E is dressed in the clothes that he had when he was warped back in time. They stare at each other.

ERICSTON

Who are you? What are you doing here?

LITTLE E

You even talk differently...I'm sorry to disturb you, sir. My name is ERICSTON WASHATON III, and everybody calls me LITTLE E. I'm your son's son.

ERICSTON

My grandson!

LITTLE E

YEAH! Your grandson...from the year 2018.

ERICSTON paces around LITTLE E looking him up and down.

LITTLE E

I know how crazy this all must sound to you. But it's the truth. I'm your grandson from the year 2018.

ERICSTON

Yes, this all sounds very crazy to me...but...

LITTLE E

But what!

ERICSTON

Your clothes, your shoes, the way you talk, those devices on your person...how? Where?

LITTLE E

That's right. You've never seen anything like these before, have you?

ERICSTON

No, I have not. How did you get here in this time?

LITTLE E

My father has a workshop in his basement or cellar as you might know it. He is a brilliant scientist and inventor, like yourself...

ERICSTON

How did you know that I am an inventor?

LITTLE E

I know that you invented the machine that will revolutionize the laundry industry. A machine that can wash and dry a ton of clothes at one time...The WASH-A-TON machine.

ERICSTON is surprised at the knowledge that LITTLE E has about him.

ERICSTON

How! How did you know?

LITTLE E

I know because old man WASHATON is going to steal the blueprints and his family will become millionaires in the future from YOUR invention. But if I could take the blueprints back with me, then all can be rectified, and the true glory can go to the rightful owners of that invention...your family.

ERICSTON

But...tell me...how you got here.

LITTLE E

I was fooling around in my father's lab when I accidentally stepped into this machine that he was working on. He warned me not to go into the lab so many times, but I had no idea he was working on something of this magnitude. (Snapping his fingers.) *The door closed behind me and...here I am!*

ERICSTON

(Shaking his head in disbelief)

Unbelievable!

LITTLE E

(Going for his wallet)

Look! Here is my driver's license, my social security card...now you know that blacks don't have social status in these times.

ERICSTON

Let me see those. (Looking very closely at the driver's license and the social security card) *So, we gain social status and are free men?*

LITTLE E

Yes, to a certain degree.

ERICSTON

What do you mean, to a certain degree?

LITTLE E

Well, we are free and gain some economic power, but the mass majority of our people are ignorant to the fact of who they are and how powerful they are.

ERICSTON

I don't understand. How can we have freedom and still remain ignorant?

LITTLE E

The "white man" hides the true history of the black man and has taken credit...just like Washaton has taken credit for your accomplishments...and reaps the benefits of our deeds. We are not recognized or even thought of as their equal.

The black people in 2018 don't have a clue as to the inventions that we have created like....

shoelaces.

LITTLE E (CONT'D)

The first brake mechanism for the trains, spoons, locks, and many parts for the automobile. I can't begin to tell you all the things that the black man has been cheated out of.

ERICSTON

Are we educated?

LITTLE E

Do you mean are we taught to read and write?

ERICSTON nods his head YES.

LITTLE E

Yes, but not the way the white man is educated.

ERICSTON

What is the difference!

LITTLE E

The difference is in the fact that the white man does not want us to advance and we are on the same or higher level than they are. It is all about power...

the power to control. They control us by pitting us against each other.

There is dissension in the black race. We fight each other and kill each other because of what has happened here, in this time. The light skinned black and the dark-skinned black are still in conflict as to which one is better. Can you believe that?

ERICSTON

So, the machines and other things that I have given to MASTER WASHATON are being sold by him, and he gives the credit to himself?

LITTLE E

And to his family!

ERICSTON

I never really thought about it much. I just like to do the drawings and think of different things that might work. MASTER WASHATON doesn't beat me like he does the others. He takes very good care of me...

LITTLE E

(Interrupting)

As long as you're up here creating things that will make him even richer than he already is! He doesn't do things for you out of the kindness of his heart. He owes everything that he has to you!

ERICSTON

Yes, yes I see what you are saying.

LITTLE E

Now is the future, it won't be as bad as things are now for the black man. A white man would get his ass kicked for striking a black man for no reason.

53

ERICSTON

You don't say!

LITTLE E

Yes, I do say! Whites are afraid of blacks, and that fear, whether imagined or real, creates a rift between the races. We are separate in thought, yet we are together physically; living in the same neighborhoods, working in the same workplace, and even going to the same recreational functions, such as the movies, clubs, and amusement parks, festivals...

LITTLE E notices the confused look on his grandfather's face.

LITTLE E

Aaa...I know that I am confusing the hell out of you granddad, but it would take me so long to tell you the complete status of the black race. (Pacing.) Let me just say that what happens here will influence the entire black race. Our children are in serious trouble.

ERICSTON

What kind of trouble?

LITTLE E

They are killing each other, and a lot of innocent people are dying as well.

ERICSTON

Why?

LITTLE E

Because we are so deprived of the finer things in life that some of our children have chosen to take what they want. They sell drugs and run around in gangs terrorizing all that cross their path. They disrespect their parents and women. They call their black queens "bitches and hoes."

They are sometimes raised by only one parent, the mother. They live in run-down and poor ghettoes and are preyed upon by every known deviate in the world. Our schools are less than second-class, and we are not taught all the knowledge that the white man has access to.

ERICSTON

Who are they teaching you about?

LITTLE E

They are teaching our children to believe that they have accomplished everything that is important; that they beat the British army all alone; that we were just slaves (uneducated animals), *that George Washington, Ethan Allen, Paul Revere, and Abraham Lincoln, just to name a few, were the only heroes.*

They never mention Dabney Austin, Edward Hector, Oliver Cromwell, or James Armistead...the list goes on.

ERICSTON

Education of ourselves is the key. We long to be treated as men.

I see my brothers and my sisters being beaten; I hear the cries and screams of my sisters as they are being ravaged by the white man. I have seen children torn from their mother's arms and taken away to be sold like cattle to another plantation.

I have seen my brothers cry because they are separated from the ones they love. I have felt the shame of my brothers and sisters as they are degraded before the eyes of the white man.

I can feel the loneliness in the barn that houses the unfortunate men and women that the only reward they seek is a swift death to ease their misery. I can hear the sadness in the songs that the SINGING SLAVE whispers through his dying soul...

ERICSTON pauses and looks intensely at LITTLE E. He touches his face as an adoring grandfather would do to a grandson.

ERICTSON (CONT'D)

I want to show you some other drawings, grandson. (He hugs LITTLE E) *See if you can recognize any of the devices?*

LITTLE E looks over the drawings. He is amazed at what he sees.

LITTLE E

Well, I'll be damned! The bicycle frame, horseshoes, a snow-melting machine, golf tees, boots, a pencil sharpener and reaper, railroad switches, a lawn sprinkler, aaa, bottles, granddad! I'm truly amazed! Your genius is astounding!!

ERICSTON

I've got many more ideas to share with you. Perhaps you can take them back to 2018 with you. By the way, how will you return home?

LITTLE E

Then you believe me that I am from the future?

ERICSTON

Of course, I do. How else can you explain the items on your person, your style of dress and your obvious knowledge of me and my inventions?

LITTLE E

Good, good. It's all good granddad! I'm glad that you don't think that I am some stark-raving mad lunatic slave from another plantation. (He looks worried.) *Although I don't know exactly how I'm getting back home, I just have to have enough faith in my father to know that he will not rest until he finds a way to get me home.*

ERICSTON

Don't worry about it, son. I have the faith to know that your father will get you back. Now, tell me more about the future.

CURTAIN

SCENE THREE

As the lights dim, LITTLE E tells his grandfather about the future.

INT: BARN - THE LIGHTS COME ON IN THE BARN - LITTLE E RUSHES IN EXCITED!

LITTLE E

I FOUND HIM!! I FINALLY FOUND MY GRANDFATHER! Ah man! He's fantastic! Brilliant! An absolute genius! I only wish that he could come here to meet you fellas and see how much you've learned.

As LITTLE E is talking, all eyes turn to the doorway behind LITTLE E. There stood a slender young black man with an armful of papers and writing tools. LITTLE E turns to see his grandfather.

LITTLE E

You came! How...?

ERICSTON

How did I sneak past everyone? Very cautiously! I felt it was about time that I met these men...my brothers.

I want to help you properly educate them, not mis-educate them as they will be taught in the future. Perhaps your returning to this time is a sign that things must be set right.

LITTLE E

RIGHT ON GRANDDAD!!

ERICSTON puts his papers down and extends his hand to NOBIE.

ERICSTON

Hello! My name is ERICSTON WASHATON. And you are?

NOBIE takes his hand and stares at him intensely.

NOBIE

My...name...is...NOBIE.

ERICSTON introduces himself to the others...TEVIN and NIC. They are delighted to know him.

TEVIN

Good eve...va...ning.

NIC

What up homey?

ERICSTON and LITTLE E laugh.

ERICSTON

Well. I see that LITTLE E has been teaching you some of the linguistics of the future.

LITTLE E

Yeah! And they are fast learners! I am so proud of the fact that they want to know more...they have a thirst for knowledge...and you can see to it that they are quenched.

ERICSTON

(Nodding his head in agreement)

Yes, yes. I will see to it that they learn all that they are capable of absorbing. I have learned much from the white man's literature. I read all the time. MR WASHATON sees to it that I have all the latest books or maps or anything that is written. I will pass this knowledge onto you all.

Everyone is happy and chatting amongst themselves.

ERICSTON

(Talking and walking around)

I will teach you to use your minds, not just your backs. I will tap inside your mental capacity and teach you to retain what you have learned. LITTLE E will help me with some of the ways of teaching from the future. This will be such a rewarding challenge for us all.

NIC

If I's...I mean I...hadn't seent ya wit my own eyes. I'd say it taint so.

TEVIN

But it tis so. I see him, too.

ERICSTON

I never felt so important before. I am a man just like all of you. I am different only because I am educated.

TEVIN

I wants to be ed...da...ca...

ERICSTON

(Interrupting)

No. The word is pronounced ed...du...ca...ted.

TEVIN

(Trying to say it properly)

Ed...du...ca...ted!

ERICSTON

Yes, yes! Very good! I know I will have to be patient with all of you and I will make sure that you understand everything that will be taught to you.

LITTLE E

Man! This is going to be so intense! I just want you all to know about so many wonderful things that it's hard to know where to begin!

ERICSTON

At the beginning!

LITTLE E

O.K., Comedian! At the beginning!

ERICSTON and LITTLE E laugh.

ERICSTON

Well. I need to get back to the attic. I will see everyone tomorrow. And tomorrow, school begins.

LITTLE E

Yeah, you had better get back before old man WASHATON misses you. I'll go back with you.

The two men situate everything and hide all the things that ERICSTON brought into the barn with him. THEY CHECK TO SEE IF IT WAS CLEAR. Since the party had died down and there were only a couple of drunken guests left, the two men saw their chance to get back into the house. LITTLE E saw to it that his grandfather made it safely to the attic.

SCENE FOUR

INT: MASTER WASHATON'S HOUSE.

On his way out of the house, LITTLE E passes by MRS. WASHATON'S room. MASTER WASHATON was passed out drunk in another part of the house, or so his wife thought. She sees LITTLE E pass by.

> **MRS. WASHATON**
> (Sitting on her bed facing the open door)

HEY, BOY!

> **LITTLE E**
> (Freezes in his tracks off stage)

YESSUM!

> **MRS. WASHATON**
> (She is slightly tipsy)

COME IN HERE!! What y'all doing in here again? Oooh! I remember you! You that good niggra slave that did me real fine! Come on in here boy.

> **LITTLE E**

But what 'bout Massa, ma'am?

> **MRS. WASHATON**
> (Frustrated)

Never mind him!! He somewhere drunk! (She motions for LITTLE E to come to her bed) *Get over here now...BOY!*

LITTLE E reluctantly enters the room.

> **MRS. WASHATON**

That's a good niggra.

LITTLE E IS DISGUSTED by MRS. WASHATON. He walks slowly to her bed with his head down. When he reaches the bed, she grabs him and pulls him on top of her. Suddenly, MASTER

WASHATON enters the room.

MASTER WASHATON

(Rushing toward the bed)

YA BITCH! WHAT DA HELL IS DAT NIGGRA DOIN' IN HERE?
I'LL KILL YA BLACK MONKEY ASS!!

MASTER WASHATON grabs LITTLE E and throws him to the floor.
LITTLE E jumps up and strikes WASHATON. MRS. WASHATON is on
the bed screaming and crying.

MRS. WASHATON

THAT NIGGRA TRIED TO HAVE HIS WAY WIT ME!!

No one is paying attention to MRS. WASHATON. During the
struggle between LITTLE E and WASHATON, LITTLE E makes a
dash for the door, but he trips and MASTER WASHATON grabs an
object, hitting LITTLE E IN THE HEAD AND KNOCKING HIM OUT.

MASTER WASHATON

I'M GONNA STRANG YA UP NIGGRA!!

MRS. WASHATON

Yeah! Yeah! Strang his black ass up!

MASTER WASHATON

SHUT UP, BITCH!

MRS. WASHATON gets quiet and humble.

Utile E's Trouble

INT: LAB IN BASEMENT OF BIG E HOME

The lights come up in the lab of BIG E. He is working at the AGGRANDIZER. He is punching in numbers at his computer board trying to come up with the right sequence to get his son home. The lights dim in the lab.

EXT: MASTER WASHATON'S YARD

The lights (red) come up in the 1800s. LITTLE E is about to be hung. It is a dark and lonely night. PERCY, MASTER WASHATON, AND SKULLY are present. PERCY whips LITTLE E with the whip that he has beaten so many other slaves with. SKULLY is enjoying what he sees.

SKULLY

Y'all goes hang dis nigga, Massa (smirking)*? Him shouda be hanged. Him ain't no nigga from 'round here no how!*

MASTER WASHATON

Shut ya fool mouth boy and hand me the rope.

SKULLY hands MASTER WASHATON the rope. He throws it over the hanging post. LITTLE E is bound and gagged, his shirt torn, his skin bleeding.

MASTER WASHATON

I'll teach ya niggras where yo true place is in this world. Y'all belong at the tip of the whip and the end of a rope. Y'all ain't nuthin' but animals and ya should be treated like 'em.

He swings around to PERCY.

MASTER WASHATON

PERCY!

PERCY

Yessa!

MASTER WASHATON

Strang this niggra up...holds 'im so I can get this rope 'round his neck.

As they go to put the rope around LITTLE E's neck, a puff of smoke comes out of nowhere. The red light goes dim, and the lights in the lab come up. LITTLE E appears in the Aggrandizer with his bloody slave clothes, dazed with the gag still around his neck. BIG E rushes to open the Aggrandizer to get his son.

BIG E

OH, MY GOD!! LITTLE E! WHAT HAPPENED SON? WHAT...

He helps LITTLE E get free of his bonds. LITTLE E is so excited.

LITTLE E

DAD! IS IT REALLY YOU? AM I REALLY HOME?

BIG E

YES, SON. YES. YOU ARE HOME! BUT YOU MUST TELL ME WHERE YOU HAVE BEEN!

LITTLE E

MAN! You will not believe! I was back in the 1800s! I met ERICSTON WASHATON! My great-great grandfather!

BIG E

(Almost speechless)

Whaaa..?

LITTLE E

Yes! Yes! ERICSTON WASHATON...and he is an absolute genius. I met TEVIN, NIC, NOBIE...and...Oh yeah...the Massa's (mocking the slaves) wife...and...and...

BIG E

WHOA! SLOW DOWN SON! Who are these people?

LITTLE E

They are...or were slaves that I met in the year 1800! Great-granddad and I were teaching them to read and write and...oh, by the way, dad, (excited) *IT WORKS! The Aggrandizer works!*

I'm sorry I disobeyed you and came snooping around down here, but I had to know what you were working on. Dad, you are a genius! Do you realize the possibilities that this could mean?

BIG E

Yes, son. I do know the possibilities, and I also know the dangers. What if I couldn't get you back? What if whoever did this to you succeeded before I had a chance to get you back? It was not a good idea for you to bother with things that you know nothing about! (Calming down) *I am just so glad that you are home and safe.*

LITTLE E

But Dad, you don't understand! I have to go back!

BIG E

Are you out of your mind?

LITTLE E

Were you out of your mind when you decided to invent this time machine?

What is the purpose if you don't use it? I mean, you (his voice picks up) <u>AND I</u> could rectify so many wrongs that have been committed against our people.

The inventions alone would be reason enough to go back in time and give credit back to our people. The white man has taken too much from us as it is. Don't let them take anymore.

You know as well as I do that if they found out about this time machine, it would no longer belong to you and they would receive all the glory for it while you and your future generations will end up with a kick in the ass or a rope around your neck!

The two men sit and stare at each other.

BIG E

You are right son, but we must be so careful. We will have to sit down <u>together</u> and devise a plan to use the Aggrandizer. But it must be tested further before another human being is catapulted in time. There may be some unforeseen side effects. I don't know yet.

LITTLE E

Don't worry Dad. We'll cross all those bridges when we get to them. But for now... (Looking into the audience) *...all I know is that the AGGRANDIZER works!*

CURTAIN

THE END — OR IS IT?